For Tricia, Van Morrison and my father
"...as big as a whale's love can be."

MY FRIEND WHALE

A Bantam Little Rooster Book/March 1991

Originally published by Walker Books Ltd., London.

Little Rooster is a trademark of Bantam Books, a division
of Bantam Doubleday Dell Publishing Group, Inc.

Library of Congress Cataloging-in-Publication Data
James, Simon.
    My friend whale/Simon James
      p. cm.
    "A Bantam little rooster book."
    Summary: A child's enjoyment of a whale in the sea
near his home ceases when the whale is never seen again.
A final page emphasizes the necessity of preserving whales.
    ISBN 0-553-07065-7
    1. Whales–Juvenile fiction.   [1. Whales–fiction.]   I. Title
PZ10.3.J274My   1990   90–194
[E]–dc20   CIP
                                 AC

Published simultaneously in the United States and Canada

Bantam Books are published by Bantam Books, a division of
Bantam Doubleday Dell Publishing Group, Inc. Its trademark,
consisting of the words "Bantam Books" and the portrayal of a
rooster, is registered in U.S. Patent and Trademark Office and
in other countries. Marca Registrada. Bantam Books, 666 Fifth
Avenue, New York, New York 10103.

PRINTED IN HONG KONG BY SOUTH CHINA PRINTING CO. (1988) LIMITED
0 9 8 7 6 5 4 3 2 1

MY FRIEND WHALE

Simon James

A BANTAM LITTLE ROOSTER BOOK
NEW YORK · TORONTO · LONDON · SYDNEY · AUCKLAND

My friend Whale and I swim together every night.

My friend Whale is a blue whale.

My friend Whale makes the biggest splash of any sea creature,

but he is a very slow and graceful swimmer.

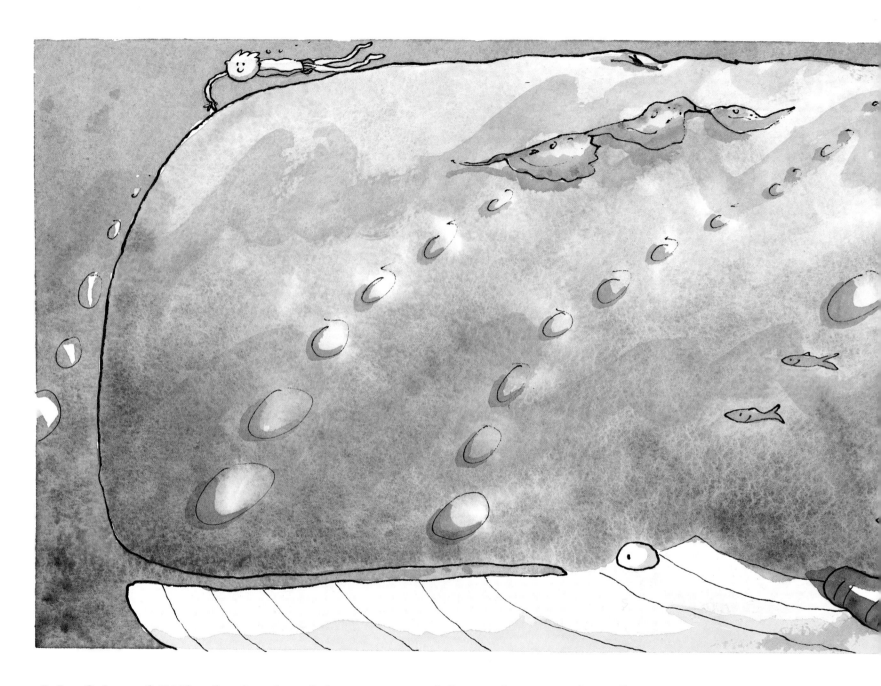

My friend Whale is the biggest and heaviest animal
on land or in the sea.

You may think, because he is so large, that he must be dangerous.

But my friend Whale has no teeth.

In fact, he only eats fishy things smaller than my little finger.

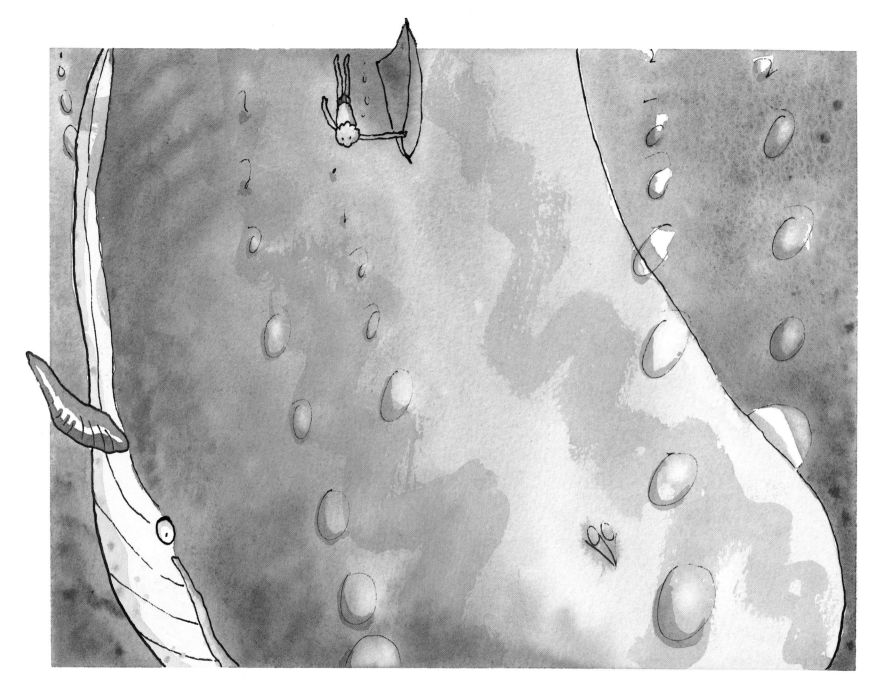

My friend Whale can hold his breath underwater for almost an hour.

But because he is not a fish, he has to come up for air just like me.

My friend Whale can't smell anything.
My friend Whale can't taste anything.

But he has very good ears –
he can hear an underwater world of things that I can't.

My friend Whale speaks with squeaking, clicking,
and whistling sounds.

Other whales can hear him from a hundred miles away.

My friend Whale has very sensitive skin.
He can feel the slightest touch.

That is the way I say good-bye for the night.
See you tomorrow, my friend Whale.

My friend Whale really does make the biggest splash. But the next night, I don't see the spray of his spout or the splash of his tail.

He didn't come for me at all.

My friend Whale didn't come last night either, or the night before. Maybe he's found a new friend.

Or maybe something has happened to him.
Now my friend Whale only visits in my dreams.